Craving the Darkness

Kelly Michelle

Illustrated by

Shellie Hensley Vickers

ISBN-13: 9798685735812

Cover design by: Kelly Michelle & Shellie Vickers

Library of Congress Control Number: 2018675309

Printed in the United States of America

Dedicated to all those who seek solace in the shadows.

"Listen to them…children of the night…what music they make!"

- Dracula

Trigger Warning: Some of the stories in this collection contain subject matter that may not be suitable for all readers. Topics such as abuse and suicide are mentioned. If you are affected by any of these things, or just need to reach out to someone, please see the list of resources found at the end of this book.

Where the dark things live,
Where the sky is black,
Once you arrive,
There's no turning back.
Where the corpses rise,
And ghostly footsteps fall,
The wicked souls heed,
A most sinister call...

...Come play....

Look for me by the willow tree,

Where the branches hang down so delicately.

I shall be there without delay,

No reason, have I, to prolong my stay.

Bid me farewell with a kiss so sweet,

Never regret that we ever did meet.

Miss me not, remember me often,

Despite my rotting away in my coffin.

Feel not despair, like mourners do.

Wherever I go, fear not, I'll find you.

Into your nightmares will I find my way,

Consumed with the thought of the games we can play.

Why are you running from what you once loved?

From below this earth, so now above.

Come to me, darling, and grant me a kiss,

Before I depart to the unknown abyss.

Let not fright consume thy heart,

Let not our souls be torn apart.

Look for me by the willow tree…

…Where I will be hanging so delicately.

Kind

Abigail looked around the bleak cemetery. It was a grey rainy day, and the autumn breeze was scattering dried up leaves all around. She was clutching a large bouquet of multicolored chrysanthemums; they were not exactly her favorite, but her late grandmother had loved them so. Her mother was crouched beside her, tidying up the area around her grandmother's newly placed tombstone. It had been several weeks since Abigail's grandmother had passed, but this was the first time she had had the nerve to visit the cemetery since the funeral. Her mother had been stopping by once a week, and today she had insisted that Abigail join her.

"Abby, baby, hand me those flowers. Just a few at a time, though; I am going to try and arrange them neatly in this tombstone vase," said her mom. Abigail began to hand her mother the flowers a few at a time. As she waited for her to request the next batch, something near the edge of the cemetery caught her eye. "What's that over there?" she asked, pointing to a shabby, blank stone sticking out of the ground. It was only about a foot tall and appeared to be crumbling. "That is one of the old, unmarked graves. Most of those were for John and Jane Does or wards of the state; people with no families to claim them," replied her mother. Abigail let out a sigh. "That's so sad. Imagine having no one to mourn you once you're gone."

"Mom, I have an idea. May I borrow a few of these flowers?" asked Abigail. Her mother smiled knowingly and nodded approval. Abigail took a few of the chrysanthemums and walked out to the desolate grave. Gently, she laid the flowers among the weeds just in front of the stone marker. "Nobody should be alone, especially when you die," she said aloud. She stood for a moment, silently paying respects, then she turned and walked back over to her grandmother's plot to finish helping her mother. After some laughter and a few tears, they said their goodbyes and left the cemetery. The rain was beginning to fall again, heavier this time. Abigail stared out the window at the passing scenery, trying to shake the eerie feeling she always seemed to get in a graveyard. Her mom always told her it was silly to be afraid; the dead cannot hurt you. They are already gone. It is the living you have to worry about.

Later that evening, Abigail's parents left to have dinner with some friends. They had invited Abigail, but she really wasn't the social type. Besides, what would she have to say to a bunch of adults? She politely declined and planned to enjoy a quiet evening at home binge watching her favorite show. With her parents gone, she could watch the big television in the living room! She gathered up some junk food and camped out on the comfiest spot on the sofa. She was two episodes in when she heard it: a slight scratching noise coming from the kitchen window.

Abigail paused the show, straining to hear the noise again. Her breath caught in her throat when she heard it. Soft scratching, as if a tree branch were hitting the window. The only problem was, there were no trees near the kitchen. "Maybe it's a cat," she said to herself. She walked slowly into the kitchen, peered around the refrigerator towards the window the noise was coming from, and saw…nothing. The noise had stopped. She walked over, looked out into the night, and saw nothing. She shook her head and let out a sigh of relief. Then she heard the scratching again. This time, it was coming from the window in the dining room.

"Okay, are birds attacking the house? This is ridiculous," she said as she walked into the dining room. The curtains were drawn, and she had lost the bravery with which she had entered the kitchen. Her mind was torn between an annoying bird and a psycho maniac being on the other side of that glass. Suddenly, the noise was coming from the living room window. She turned and ran back through the kitchen, stopping at the doorway to look ahead and ensure that the front door was locked and bolted. It was. She wanted to yell or scream, maybe to scare whoever was out there away…but what if that just made them try harder to get in? Her cell phone was lying on the couch. She made a mad dash for it, ran back to the kitchen doorway, and called the local police.

As she gave the dispatcher her information, she hurried through the house to check that every door was locked and no windows had been opened. The scratching kept moving from one window to another randomly. She was in tears at this point, and had never felt more grateful than when she heard the sirens outside. After a few moments, she heard a loud bang on the door and a man shouted, "Police department! Are you alright?" The dispatcher confirmed to her it was indeed an officer at her door, so she hung up and ran to open it. Before she could stop herself, she threw her arms around the officer and began to sob. "I was so scared! Who was it? Did you catch them?" The officer gently pulled away from her and told her everything was going to be okay, then he called a female officer over to go inside with Abigail and take her statement.

Abigail described the scratching, how it moved randomly from window to window. The house was secure, and the police found no evidence that anyone or anything had been outside. They told her they would ride by throughout the night. They had already spoken to her parents and they were already on their way home. The responding officers left her their contact information and made one more lap around the house and yard before leaving. Thankfully, her parents' car was coming down the road as the officers pulled out of her driveway.

Abigail shut and locked the door, no reason to take any chances. Her parents had a key. She wiped a stray tear from her cheek and walked over to the couch. She gathered up her junk food and was putting it away in the kitchen when her parents came in. After tight hugs and a thousand questions, she retreated to her bedroom. Abigail flicked on the light switch, took two steps in, and stopped. She could feel her mind begin to break as it tried to explain what she was seeing. Lying on her bed, just below her pillow…was a handful of chrysanthemums.

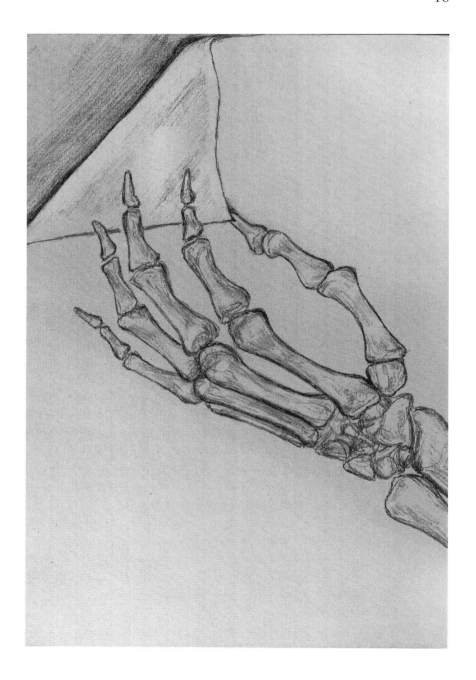

Would you miss me if I died today?

Would you notice if I went away?

If someone asked you who I was,

I wonder what you'd have to say.

Though you see me when I'm smiling,

Do you see me when I'm crying?

Do you realize, even though I look okay,

Inside I'm dying?

There's emptiness inside my heart.

A blackness that consumes my soul.

There are feelings deep inside me that

I fear the world may never know.

All who let me slip to darkness,

All who let me fall away,

Someday I will haunt your soul,

And upon your heart, my demons will play.

Carnival

Tavia stood in line for the Ferris wheel, glancing around nervously. Her friends should have been here by now. The text message said they were on their way from the ticket booth, so she should grab them a spot in line. She would certainly be in the next batch of riders, so what would she do if it were her turn to get on and they weren't there? If she left the line, people would think she was afraid to ride. Her only alternative was to ride alone, like a complete loser. She checked her phone, but for some odd reason she had no signal so close to the huge contraption. Lovely. They could be trying to reach her now and she had no idea. Stupid phone.

"Next!" Tavia looked up to see the carnival employee beginning to load people onto the ride again as others were exiting. Great, no way her friends would show up in the next 20 seconds, so she was pretty much riding alone like a lame-o. The carnival guy opened the little gate on the side of the car, letting the three occupants step off. Tavia stood awkwardly, hoping he would just shut the gate and start the ride. No such luck. "Hey, girlie! You gettin' on, or what? We ain't got all day." Her face burned with a crimson flush of embarrassment as she slowly walked up to the car and climbed in. She sat down and stared down at her feet, afraid to look and see people laughing at her. That's when she heard a guy's voice say, "Hey, hold up!"

When she looked up, a gorgeous guy had climbed into the car with her, directly across from her seat. Tavia didn't recognize him, but he sure was attractive. Obviously, he had mistaken her for someone else. "I guess you thought I was someone you knew," Tavia said softly. He laughed as a smile crossed his lips. "Nah, I just felt it was a travesty for a girl like you to be riding alone. You seem too sweet for that." Tavia blushed immediately. Was he seriously talking about her? This had to be a prank or something, right? He was clearly a few years older than her, so why would he want to ride with her? Why would he care if she were alone? "My friends were supposed to ride with me, I swear. They just didn't make it to the line in time," she muttered.

"That's okay. My friends didn't make it in time, either," he said with a smile. "I'm Matt, by the way." He extended his hand to her as the Ferris wheel began to pick up pace. She slowly grasped it with her own. "I'm Tavia."

The ride must have been fully loaded now because they began to make full circles. Tavia remarked how beautiful the city skyline was in the dark distance. Matt agreed. "You get an amazing view from here, that's for sure. If this were the last thing you ever saw, it wouldn't be such a bad way to go. Don't you think?" His remark made Tavia nervous for a moment. What an odd thing to say. Her face must have betrayed her thoughts because Matt relented. "Sorry, I don't mean to scare you. It was just one of those thoughts, you know?" His smile relaxed her, and they sat in content silence for a minute or so.

Tavia was so lost in the moment, she had forgotten about her friends completely. Matt was so good looking, and so sweet. He really seemed to be looking out for her, especially not letting her ride alone like a total spaz. As the ride brought their car to the very top, Tavia leaned over the side to get a look at how high they were. Matt grabbed her so suddenly, it startled her. "Don't do that," he said flatly. Tavia sat frozen for a few seconds, unsure how to respond. Matt's grip on her loosened slightly, and when her eyes met his she felt he was staring right through her. "O-okay. Sorry. I was just curious…" her voice trailed off. Matt smiled again. "Don't be curious. I like you too much to see you do anything dumb." Tavia's cheeks felt like they were on fire now. He liked her? He only just met her! "My friends aren't going to believe this. Do you want to help me find them when we get off the ride?" Her heart sank a little when she saw his expression darken. "Your friends…how friendly can they be? They weren't here. Why would they just ignore you like that?" Now she felt confused. "Oh, they didn't ignore me. They just got delayed or something. I promise, they're really nice. Maybe my friends can meet your friends?" Matt looked out over the horizon. "They didn't make it in time."

They sat in silence. Tavia began to feel bad for Matt. He was so nice, and had been nothing but friendly to her. She couldn't imagine his friends not showing up to hang out. How could anyone not want to be around him? Below, the carnival worker was letting people off and loading in the next crowd. Tavia tried to think of something quick to say, in case Matt took off after the ride was over. "Thank you for riding with me, Matt," she said with a smile. Matt smiled back. "Nobody should have to ride alone, Tavia." When he said her name, she felt giddy. Finally, their car reached the loading platform. The carnival guy opened the gate and Tavia hopped down, eager to find her friends and introduce them to Matt. As she walked to the stairs, she saw her friends standing off to the side. "There they are!" Tavia exclaimed, waving. She took the steps quickly. "Come on, Matt!" Halfway between her friends and the ride, she turned. Matt was gone. She looked for him in the crowd, but he wasn't there. She looked back to the Ferris wheel car they had been in, but another group was in it now. "Oh, no…" she said softly to herself.

"Sorry we're late! We got held up in the ticket line behind some crazy lady paying with change," said her friend Diane. "You didn't have to ride alone, did you? God that would be so embarrassing." Tavia shrugged. "No, I mean…I almost had to…but this guy hopped on with me at the last minute. He was nice. I wanted y'all to meet him, but I guess he took off after the ride was over. He was just being kind to me, I suppose." Diane's older brother Pete threw his arm playfully around Tavia. "Good thing you had someone with you. That ride is haunted." Diane rolled her eyes. "Oh, Pete! Shut up! That is such bullshit, and you know it." Pete turned to face them, blocking their way. "No, seriously, it is. A few years ago, before Tavia moved here, some guy died on that ride." Diane and Tavia exchanged looks. "Yes, some guy died. Doesn't make it haunted," said Diane. Tavia couldn't help but be curious. "What happened?" Diane let out an exasperated sigh of non-belief. "Some dude got all depressed and did a swan dive off the top of the Ferris wheel. The police said he had written notes to his friends, about how no one should be alone like he was and how he wanted to end it all, but by the time

they realized he was serious, it was too late. They tried to stop

him, but they just didn't make it in time." Tavia felt a lump

forming in her throat. "Wh-who was he? What was his name?"

she asked. Pete looked upward in thought. "Um…I don't

remember. Mike, or maybe….Matt. Yeah, it was some guy

named Matt."

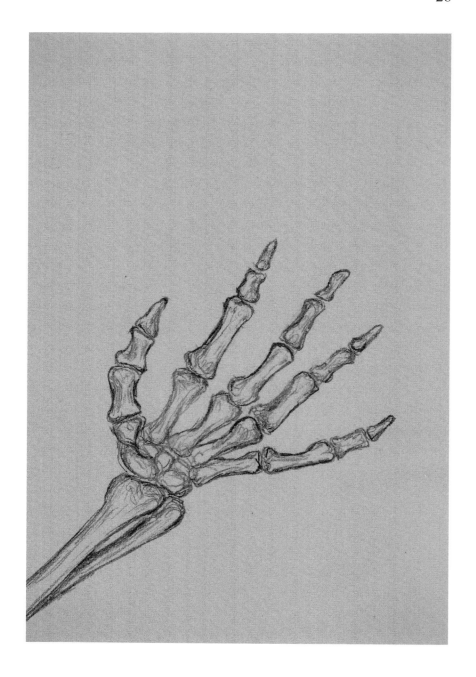

Cradle me in your arms, sweet Death.

Take me to a quiet place,

And cover me with your tattered shroud.

Cloak my vision in darkness,

Grasp my throat,

And I shall never make a sound.

Cold and pale are your hands,

Wrapping around the necks of the damned,

As you caress them with silence,

And the velvet black of night.

Softly, you ease me into slumber,

And steal my soul without a fight.

Estate

Claudia hurriedly made her way up the front walk to the quaint little house. She was running late, and as she walked she was flipping through the stack of paperwork in the estate file folder she'd brought with her. She was normally more prepared for an estate tour prior to listing, but her coworker had had a sudden emergency and had begged her to step in today. She was unfamiliar with the property, the current owners, or any details of the surrounding neighborhood. Right in front of the steps leading to the porch, her distraction got the best of her. She stumbled, catching herself on the railing but letting go of the folder in the process. Papers flew all over the front porch. "Oh, shoot!" Claudia was so embarrassed. Hopefully the new client hadn't witnessed her tumble.

After she gathered herself and her paperwork, Claudia looked for the doorbell. There did not seem to be one, as was sometimes the case with these older houses, so she knocked. That is when she realized the front door was slightly ajar. "Hello? Is anyone home? I'm from the realtor's office," Claudia called out.

"Oh, do come in dear," said a soft voice. Opening the door wider, Claudia saw an elderly lady standing just inside the foyer, dusting a small table that held keys and mail. "I went out to sweep the porch earlier, and I suppose I didn't shut that door all the way. You say you are from the realtor's office?" asked the woman.

"Yes," replied Claudia. "My coworker Gayle is the actual agent handling things, but she had an emergency and asked me to come by and do the initial tour of the home and grounds. My name is Claudia. Who might you be?" The old lady smiled warmly. "My name is Emma Johnson. This is my home. It's been in the family for many years, but now there's no one to take care of the place. I never married, or had any children, so there's no one to pass it on to. It's time to let it go to a more capable owner. I'm at peace with that." Claudia smiled, but she felt a slight sadness for the woman. Reaching the age where you have to let go of your home must be difficult.

"I apologize, but I am not very well prepared for our tour today. This was asked of me quite last minute, I'm afraid. From what I read here, your estate is handling the sale?" Claudia asked, looking up from her folder. "I suppose. I'm just a simple old woman, no head for business and such. My brothers always handled those things for me when they were still around. I'm afraid no one else is home, but I will be more than happy to show you the house," replied Emma. Claudia nodded, and followed Emma as she walked towards the formal living room.

As they walked from one room to the next, Claudia began to relax. This was a beautiful home, filled with such a rich history. Emma was a delightful lady, and each room brought forth an entertaining tale from her life. The house itself did not seem to be in need of very much repair, just a good cleaning. It was a bit dusty, as though it hadn't been lived in for a few months. Claudia didn't mention it, though. Emma had said she was hoping to sell to a capable owner, so no doubt her age was keeping her from cleaning the place properly. Claudia didn't want to risk embarrassing her. As they neared the end of the tour, Claudia felt almost sad. Emma reminded her of a favorite aunt she had known growing up, and she had been enjoying hearing Emma's stories and laughter.

"I suppose that's all I have to show you, dear. Sorry if I rambled a bit about days gone by. It's been lonely here, and you seem like such a sweet young lady," said Emma. She smiled, and so did Claudia. "No, don't apologize. I enjoyed every minute of this. You've had quite a colorful life, Ms. Johnson." Emma shook her head, "Please, call me Emma, dear." As she walked towards the front door, Claudia found herself concerned about Emma's fate once the house was sold. Would she be alright? Where would she go? "Emma? I know selling your home must be difficult. You're going to be okay, aren't you?" Emma gave a gentle nod. "I'll be fine, don't you worry. I have enough memories to last forever, and this place deserves love and care beyond my years." Claudia smiled, thanked Emma for her time, and assured her that Gayle would be in touch in a day or two. As she started down the steps, she opened the folder again to review the main documents. Then, she turned back with a brilliant idea: "Emma? I really enjoyed your company today, and your stories. I would love to spend time with you again, outside of the real estate matters. Would you mind if I visited you sometime?" A genuine grin spread across Emma's face. "Why, that would be lovely! You are always welcome, dear." "Great," said Claudia. "Why don't I take you out for tea this Saturday?" Emma's smile faded. "Oh, I'm afraid I can't do that." Claudia felt a little embarrassed at her eagerness to take up this woman's time. Had she mistaken politeness for some sort of bond? "Of course, I'm sure you have a lot to do regarding the sale," Claudia replied, looking once more at the estate information. "No, it isn't that, dear. I just haven't been able to leave the house since the funeral." As she spoke these words, Claudia's eyes fell upon the word stamped below 'Emma Johnson – owner' on the paperwork: ***DECEASED.***

Rock-a-bye baby,

I'll sing you a song.

From a day filled with friends,

To a nighttime alone.

Do you really hear me?

Or am I in your head?

Could I be the shadow,

At the foot of your bed?

Hush little baby,

Please don't cry.

No one will answer,

When you ask "why?"

Why were you left here,

To cry all alone?

Will no one come save you?

Is nobody home?

No daddy to love you,

Or sing lullabies.

No mommy to wipe away

Tears from your eyes.

The bough is broken,

And the cradle fell.

You poor little thing.

The fear must be hell.

So, hush little baby.

Close your eyes.

Push away the world.

It's a world full of lies.

Give in to your fear.

It's the only thing true.

Fall into the darkness.

I'm waiting for you.

Soon

This cabin is uncomfortably quiet. It is already dark out, and all I have is the moonlight streaming in through a few of the windows. Of course I would end up in the older style cabin with no electricity. Yes, I could build a fire, but that is not one of my natural skills. No doubt, I would burn the place down. I will just make do. Besides, they will be back soon. I will be alright until then. I look around at the blackness creeping out from the corners. The shadows seem to be dancing in delight. Earlier events play out again in my mind. I close my eyes.

Screams. First, I remember the screams. Those always seem to come back before anything else. Hearing a person scream out in true terror is a sound unlike any other. You never forget it. One would think you'd become numb to it after a while, but you don't. I often wonder what goes through a person's mind when they are at the point of hysterical screaming? I really shouldn't be thinking about these things. Here I am, sat silently in a darkened cabin in the woods. Do I really want to ponder the macabre? Wait, is that a car? Are they home? No. False alarm.

I glance at my watch. It is getting kind of late. Should I be worried? No, everything is fine. They'll be home soon. This place is bigger than I expected. Sparsely decorated, though. Not much besides two beds and a table with four chairs. If I needed to hide, where would I go? If there were to be more than four guests, where would they sit? This cabin wasn't very well planned, as far as vacation spots go. Of course, it is extremely remote. Ideal for one person or a couple. However, cramming three people into this space was just asking for someone to end up very uncomfortable.

I take a deep breath, trying to relax in the shadows. I feel tense, now. Crowded, even though this cabin is mostly bare. I exhale, attempting to drown out the screams in the back of my mind. Right now, there is only peace and quiet. I should enjoy this. I feel a slight movement by my feet. Sighing, somewhat dramatically, I look down. Her eyes are almost bulging in horror.

No doubt, more of those delicious screams reside behind the thick layer of duct tape over her mouth. I lean down and give her a gentle smile, holding my index finger to my lips. We must remain silent and still, lest we give away our presence. I see her try, to no avail, to wiggle loose from the ropes. Fire building may not be a skill of mine, but knot tying certainly is. I sit back up straight, tighten my grasp around the knife, and continue my wait. They'll be home soon.

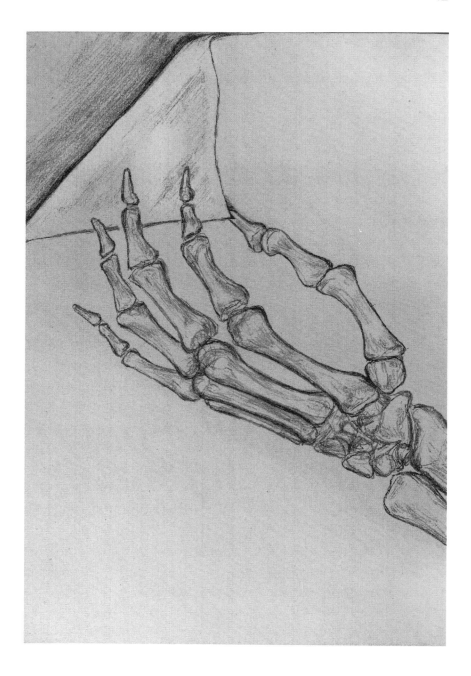

Staring at the body laid out before me,

His eyes cloaked beneath eyelids never again to open,

I shut my own as tightly as I can.

Is this what eternity looks like?

In my mind's eye, I see a white mist approaching.

Like wisps of smoke, two ghostly arms encircle my waist.

A chill makes it way up my spine, to the base of my neck.

The faintest whisper says, "Come to me."

My eyes open instantly; the light is momentarily blinding.

I see the body. The body hasn't moved.

I stand alone in the room.

Is that laughter?

Him

He was so incredibly handsome. Gabrielle stood in awe of him. How could a man possess such striking features? How was it even possible? She walked quietly to his side. Her gaze fell upon his thick, black hair. It was slightly disheveled. "Sweet boy, let me fix that," she said softly. She reached for a comb from the table next to them. His eyes were closed tightly. "I'll be gentle." She delicately began to comb through his wavy mane. "You are so handsome, and I cannot believe you are finally mine." Gabrielle had known him for many years. Since the eighth grade, in fact. He'd never really noticed her before, though. In their senior year, he'd signed her yearbook with the generic 'Have a nice summer' and his signature. That was all different now, though. He was here and he was hers.

Gabrielle placed the comb back upon the table. She began to lightly stoke his cheek. Such smooth skin. She wished he would wake up so she could tell him everything that was in her heart at that very moment. She didn't want to disturb him, though. No, she would be as quiet as a mouse, and simply enjoy being close to him. "I wonder what you are thinking, my love," she whispered as she continued stroking his cheek. She couldn't help but fixate on his lips. The lips she had dreamed of kissing for the last decade. She used to daydream in class about his lips. She'd watched him kissing his date at the senior prom and been so jealous. Now she was the one who had those lips.

Gabrielle leaned down, just above him. Her breath was slight upon his face. Still caressing his cheek, she silently took in the sight of him. She couldn't believe he was here, with her, and all her teenage dreams were becoming reality. Touching his skin, running her fingers through his jet black hair, and being so close that she could inspect every detail of his face and body. That Adonis body! Gabrielle could no longer resist, so she softly pressed her lips to his. She breathed in his scent as she felt the pressure of his mouth against her own. She was losing herself in this kiss. She loved him so. She felt as though she might give in to other desires. Suddenly the silence was broken. "Gabrielle? Are you down there?"

The shouting voice brought her back to her senses. Her boss was coming down the stairs. "Gabby? What are you doing? Are you almost done? Is he ready?" Gabrielle quickly moved away from him, collecting herself. "Y-yes! All done! He's ready!" Her boss nodded. "Good. The family has begun to arrive for the viewing, and the funeral starts in an hour. Help me get him into the casket."

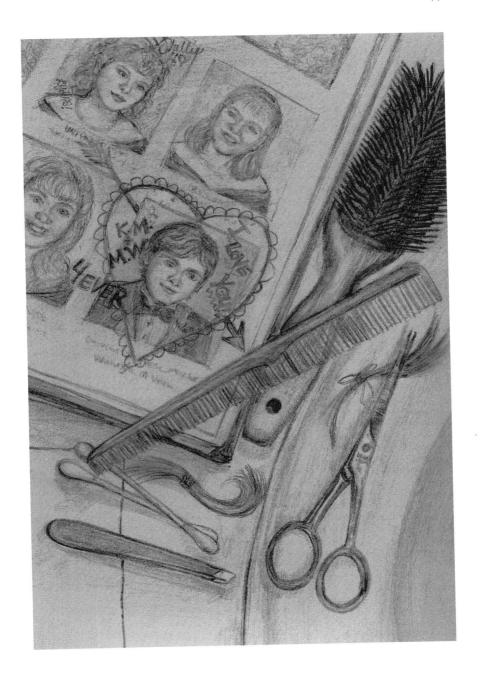

I lie in the dark,

My eyes shut tightly.

The sweet hush of night,

Is broken by unknown voices.

I can hear them,

Just outside my door,

Their muffled whispers,

And the strange laughter of a child.

Oh, what horrible things,

Might await me,

Out there in the shadows?

I dare not open my eyes.

Suddenly, all seems quiet,

And the noises fade away.

I catch my breath and relax.

The tension leaves my body,

And I feel warm and safe again.

But then, the sound of the door opening,

Pierces the silence.

Mischief

April ran out of the house in an absolute panic. Tears were streaming down her face, and she could hardly catch her breath. Why had she been so stupid? Just because her friends were foolish enough to play around with a Ouija board, why did she have to follow along? She was terrified as she ran down the street and towards her own house. Grandmother had always warned her not to mess with Ouija boards. "They are a gateway to terrible things," she had said. Her words rang loudly in April's ears now. She just wanted to be in her home, safe in bed, where nothing could get to her.

She burst through the front door so suddenly that her mother let out a scream. "April? Honey, what are you doing home? I thought you were sleeping over at Rylan's tonight?" Her mother looked both sympathetic and confused as April threw her arms around her. "Oh, mama! It was awful! I'm so sorry," she sobbed. Her mother sat her down on the couch and tried to wipe away her tears. "Sweetheart! What happened? Please tell me," she pleaded. April began to recount her experience. She told her mother how some of the other girls brought a Ouija board, and how Rylan kept urging her to join them. They wanted to summon a spirit. April knew it was dangerous. Grandmother had always been adamant against it. Still, they were her friends. She was safe, right?

"Wrong! I was so wrong, mama! The lights went out, and one of the other girls started to talk in a weird voice! Then a vase broke all by itself," April stammered. "I swear I saw a huge shadow moving along the wall towards me, so I grabbed my bag and ran!" She buried her face in her mother's embrace and cried even harder. "Oh, honey. I know it was scary, but I feel like maybe those girls were just playing a prank on you. Maybe we should call Rylan's parents and find out what is going on?" April shook her head. "No, please don't. A prank? Why would anyone be so mean? No, no mama. Don't call. If it was real, I don't want anything to do with it. If it was a prank, then…" her voice trailed off. Several more hugs from her mother, and the reinstitution of her old night light, and April sound asleep in her own bed.

The next morning, she awoke with a start. Had last night really happened? Was she okay? She quickly looked around her room. No monsters, nothing out of the ordinary. She got dressed and headed downstairs. After breakfast, she made her way over to the town library to return some books. The day was pleasant enough. She was almost able to forget the terrible fright she'd had the night before. That was, until she saw Rylan and two of the other girls heading towards her on the sidewalk. April tensed up, afraid of a possible negative confrontation. Rylan spoke first. "Hi, April. Are you alright?" She seemed genuinely concerned, which confused April a bit. "I guess so," she replied. Rylan glanced between the other two girls. "Look, last night was supposed to be fun. Some of the other girls decided to prank us. I swear, I didn't know. They faked the whole séance thing. I promise I didn't mean for you to get scared." April stood quiet for a moment, trying to take it all in. "So none of it was real? No one was possessed?" "No, they were just being mean," replied Rylan.

Normally, April would have been hurt and wanted to just run away, but Rylan seemed very sincere in her apology. Also, the other two girls agreed that they didn't find the prank at all funny. Forgiveness was granted, and all four of them went off to the local ice cream shop for a few cones. The rest of the afternoon ended up being one of the best April had enjoyed in quite some time. When she got home, her mother was pleased to see a positive change in her demeanor. "You sure look happy! How was your afternoon?" April began to recount the events of her day, including how the Ouija séance was fake. "You were right mom; it was a mean prank. Rylan wasn't in on it, though," she added. She wondered aloud if her grandmother had exaggerated about Ouija boards and bad things. Her mom let out a slight chuckle. "Your grandmother was what we call 'eccentric.' She believed in a lot of strange things; that doesn't make them true. You've got no cause to worry, sweetie. Now go wash up for dinner."

April bounded up the stairs and into the bathroom. As she was drying her hands, she decided to change her shirt. They were having pasta with sauce tonight, and this shirt was one of her favorites. April wasn't about to risk a stain. She grabbed a comfy t-shirt from the closet and quickly swapped it with the sweater she had worn all day. She walked over to the mirror to check herself, when suddenly the lights flickered. Was there a storm tonight? She looked out the window, but the weather was clear. April shrugged and looked back into the mirror. Standing behind her in the reflection was a ghastly, disturbing creature. Her grandmother's warnings flooded back into her mind. A demon. The lights went out. April could hear her mother calling her for dinner. April never answered.

I stood still in the darkness,

A cool breeze swept around me,

Wrapping me in its chilling, ghostly grasp,

Like the hand of a dead man.

My eyes shut tightly,

I held my breath;

Listening for the faintest whisper,

To prove I was not alone.

Friend

The sun was warm and inviting. The field had begun to bloom with the flowers of spring. Cori sat alone on a huge rock, playing with her stuffed bear, Ruffles. He was named after her father's favorite chips. Cori's family had just moved to this town, and she didn't have any friends here. There were still a few months left of school, and she missed her old classmates back home. Things felt too tense around the new house, so she often played out in this huge field by herself. She dreamed of making a friend, but she was too shy to approach any of the girls in her class.

"I guess we better head home soon, Ruffles," she said aloud. That's when she heard a soft voice ask, "Who's Ruffles?" Cori turned around and saw a small girl standing by the base of the rock. She looked to be about the same age as Cori, give or take a year. "Who are you?" asked Cori. The little girl smiled. "I'm Daphne. My family lives just over that hill at the edge of the field." Cori looked at her with slight unease. "How come I've never seen you before? Don't you have to go to school?" The little girl nodded. "Oh, yes. My mom teaches me." She paused for a second, and with a sad look, added, "I don't really have any friends." Daphne looked down at the ground.

Cori understood how she was feeling. "I don't really have any friends, either. I am new in town, we just moved into that old house over on Braycott Lane." Cori said. "I know that place. I went trick-or-treating there one Halloween," replied Daphne. Then she perked up and said, "Let's be friends! What's your name?" Cori smiled and introduced herself. Daphne joined her on the rock and Cori began to tell her the history of Ruffles. Daphne gave him a squeeze. "He's so soft!" she proclaimed. After a while, Cori got down from the rock. "I'm sorry, Daphne, but I have to be home for dinner or my momma will get upset with me." Daphne nodded and hopped down as well. "Want to meet here tomorrow after school?" asked Daphne. Cori let a huge grin spread across her face. "Sure!" They said their goodbyes, and Cori hurried home for dinner.

The next afternoon, Cori couldn't wait to get out to the field. She was practically running on her way out the door, Ruffles in hand. "Cori? Where are you going?" asked her mother. "To the field to play with Daphne! She's the girl I told you about last night." Her mom gave an approving smile. "Be home in time for dinner." When Cori got to the field, Daphne was already waiting on the rock. She was holding a tattered, stuffed rabbit. "Hi Cori!" she exclaimed. "This is Sir Fluff. I thought he and Ruffles should meet." The two girls played and talked for hours, until it was time for Cori to leave for dinner. As they walked out of the field, Cori turned towards Daphne. "Want to come over to my house tomorrow? It's Saturday, so I don't have school. Do you?" Cori asked. Daphne shook her head. "No, no school for me, either. I'll come over after breakfast." The two girls hugged and Cori ran home for dinner.

Cori was helping clear the breakfast dishes when she heard a knock at the door. Her mom was busy in the kitchen, so she went to see who it was. She wasn't supposed to open the door herself, but she saw it was Daphne. Mom hadn't seemed to hear

her knock, so Cori figured it was okay to let her in herself.

"Come on in! Let's go play in my room!" Cori said. The two girls

ran upstairs and became lost in imaginative play. Cori showed

Daphne pictures of her old neighborhood, and Daphne told her

stories about some of the people from this new town. They must

have gotten a little loud, because after a while her mom came in.

"Cori, what is all this noise? What are you doing up here?" she

said.

"Sorry momma, I was just playing with Daphne. She

came by after breakfast. We didn't mean to be so loud." Cori said

apologetically. Her mom looked around, smiled, and said, "Just

keep it down, okay?" She turned to walk out, and almost as an

afterthought, she said over her shoulder, "Bye, Daphne." The two

girls erupted into giggles as the door went closed. Over the next

several weeks, Cori and Daphne played together. Sometimes at

Cori's house, and other times around town. They never went to

Daphne's house, though. Daphne had said her parents didn't

appreciate company. Cori got the feeling that maybe they were not so nice. Lately, her own parents had seemed to change. They fought a lot, and whenever Cori asked to go play with Daphne, they seemed irritated. Her dad had said to her last week that he thought maybe she was spending too much time with Daphne. How could having a friend be a bad thing?

The girls were playing in Cori's room one day when her mother rushed in. "Cori, I have a headache. Can you *please* keep the noise down?" she said angrily. Cori shrank a little. "Sorry, momma. We will be more quiet." Suddenly her mother looked around the room. "We? What do you mean *we*? YOU were making that noise!" she yelled. Cori didn't understand her mom's frustration with her, so she tried to appease her. "Sorry, momma. We will go outside and play. Come on, Daphne." Cori and Daphne stood up to leave, and her mother grabbed Cori by the shoulders. "Stop it! Stop this nonsense! I have had enough! There is NO DAPHNE!" screamed her mother. Cori's eyes grew wide. "Momma, what do you mean? She's right there!" Cori cried. Her

mother turned towards Daphne, but didn't seem to look *at* her.
"No! You have carried on this silly game long enough! There is
nobody here! Now stop talking to yourself and grow up! I have
had it with your nonsense!" Her mother turned and stormed out
of the room. Cori stood there, horrified. Why couldn't her mother
see Daphne? "I should go now," Daphne said softly. She walked
out the door, and Cori heard her go down the stairs. Then she
heard the front door open and shut. She ate alone in her room that
night, and cried herself to sleep.

Weeks passed and Cori didn't hear from Daphne. She
wanted to go look for her, but her mother had grounded her after
that terrible day. When her restriction was finally lifted, Cori
made a beeline for the field. There was no sign of Daphne. She
sat on their rock, thinking. Daphne's parents had never sounded
like nice people, so maybe Daphne was in trouble? Cori
remembered Daphne saying she lived in the old blue house at the
edge of the field. Cori had only seen it from a distance, but today
she was determined to rescue her friend! She hopped off the rock

and, along with trusty Ruffles, headed towards the farthest edge of the field.

As she got within a few feet of the property, she could just see the top of the old blue house. It seemed pretty quiet, so she began to take her steps carefully. She didn't want to draw too much attention and risk getting Daphne in trouble. She walked closer to the old house, and noticed that it looked very run down. "Poor Daphne, this place is awful." she said aloud to herself. From behind a tree, she took a brave peek at the front door. Only, there wasn't one. The doorway stood wide open. That's when Cori noticed there were no windows. Well, there were windows in the house, but they had no glass. "This place looks abandoned, Ruffles." Cori said.

Cori finally got enough courage to walk up to the porch. She could see inside the house; it was empty. She decided to go inside. There were a few random pieces of furniture, some trash strewn about, and rag-like tatters of old curtains, but nobody lived here. Cori's heart sank. 'Daphne must live in a place even worse than this, and she didn't want me to know.' Cori thought. That's when Cori heard a woman wailing, like a violent shriek, coming from somewhere inside the empty home. She ran out of the house as fast as her young legs would carry her. Across the weed-filled yard, and into the thicket of trees on the edge of the property. She was running so fast and so fearfully, she tripped on an unseen object. Cori hit the ground hard, knocking her wind away for a brief moment. She looked back to see what had tripped her. There, beneath the dirt and the leaves, was a small stone sticking up from the ground. Cori crawled over to get a better look. It was a small, handmade grave marker. It bore the name "Cyprus Mitchell." Cori knew Daphne's last name was Mitchell. Was this a relative? Then she noticed another stone nearby. She pulled herself up off the ground and walked over to the next stone. "Agnes Mitchell," Cori read out loud. There was some smaller print. "Mother to Daphne," read Cori. She didn't understand. Daphne was an orphan? Who did she live with?

Cori tightened her grip on Ruffles and decided to just get out of there as quick as possible. She had only taken a few steps towards the woods when she tripped over something else. "Really?" she exclaimed. She looked down, and saw yet a third small stone at her feet. It was covered in dirt. In front of it was an old, dirty stuffed animal. A rabbit. "Sir Fluff?" Cori asked. Cori looked back at the grave marker. She reached down and dusted it off with her hand. Her eyes began to well up and her lips trembled as she read the inscription aloud: "Daphne Mitchell, child of Agnes. Drowned in the Holstead River. 1887-1895."

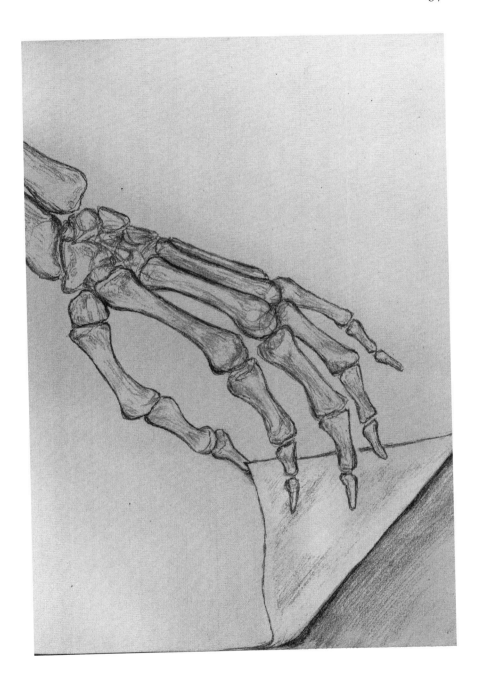

Miss me when I've left this place,

Spread my ashes upon the ground.

Shed no tears, and feel no sorrow,

For I, my dear, can still be found.

I'm afraid I have succumbed to evil,

Cruelty, and bitter revelations.

I have given in to darkness,

And its powers of persuasion.

My thoughts are now quite devious,

My heart within is frozen,

And no one can release me,

From the path that I have chosen.

Demons dance inside my mind,

Behind these eyes so hollow,

The devils seem to call to me,

And I am apt to follow.

Miss me, but don't wish me back.

Fan not the flames of that fire,

For I just might possess your soul,

To consummate my wicked desires.

Notes

John was never close to his grandmother. In fact, the old woman had irritated him more than anything. She always seemed to favor his younger sister. No matter what John accomplished in life, that woman never seemed pleased. Now, here he sat at her funeral, trying to mask the fact that he didn't feel particularly sad like everyone else. The priest was saying something, and then everyone's head was bowed for a prayer. John looked around the group at the graveside. All these people acting like she was some kind of saint, and apparently only he knew the truth. Wretched, hateful old woman that she was. Good riddance.

The graveside service came to a close, and people began to drift about, hugging each other and offering sympathy. John was unable to escape the cemetery without speaking to a few relatives. They meant well, but hearing sweet memories about this woman was difficult for him. She had everyone fooled, apparently. As he made it to his car, he heard his younger sister calling after him. John turned to see her hurrying to his side.

"John, are you okay?" He rolled his eyes. "Why wouldn't I be?" His reply made her frown. "John, don't be like that. She loved you just as much as she did every one of us," his sister stated emphatically. John let out a slight laugh. "She did, huh? So she constantly put you down and told you how you could be better? No, sis, she actually *loved* you. All I ever got was her disdain. You got the affection and the support. I was never good enough…" his voice trailed off. John's sister hugged him tightly. "I'm sorry you feel that way. I suppose I will see you at the will reading next Tuesday?" She looked up at his face, searching for a yes. John let out a sigh. "Yes, I'll be there. Happy?"

The reading of the will was being carried out at his grandmother's estate. John had hoped they could do this at the lawyer's office; he had no desire to set foot back in this house. Too many bad memories. He walked into the parlor to find his sister, mother, and two uncles already there. 'Vultures,' thought John. The lawyer arrived and they all settled down for the reading. As he had expected, the house went to his mother. The money was divided between his mother and the two uncles. A special financial provision was made for his sister. She also got some of the art work, a few antiques, and some jewelry. John got nothing. This, he had also expected. His mother and sister had the audacity to act shocked. "Can I go now?" John asked. The lawyer nodded, and John stood and headed for the door.

As he was putting on his coat in the hallway, his sister joined him. Locking her arm into his, she began to walk with him out the door and towards his car. "John, you do know she loved you, right?" John just stared straight ahead. His sister continued to speak. "Look, I know she wasn't so warm to you, but if you want anything that she left me I will gladly share." John shook his head. "No. I don't want anything from her or from this house. I didn't expect anything, and I am glad not to have been given anything. The sooner she vanishes from my life, the better off I'll be." As he said this, he realized he was being insensitive to his sister's grief. "I'm sorry, sis. I know you loved her a lot. I just didn't have the same relationship with her. But I am here for you if you need me, okay?" She turned and looked up at him. "Thank you. I miss her, John. I keep expecting her to call or something. I keep hoping for some sign that she is still around." John shook his head. "A sign? What kind of sign?" he asked. His sister smiled, tears forming in her eyes. "She always told me to listen for the music. If she wanted to let me know she was around, I would hear music. You know she and I always used to play the piano together, right? Music was kind of our thing. So, I just keep listening for the music and hoping she will let me know she is here."

John had to stifle his laughter. He didn't want to upset his sister any further. He hugged her tightly, kissed her cheek, and drove away. Walking into his apartment forty-five minutes later, he felt a huge sense of relief. This horrible week and a half was finally over, and he could get back to living his life. That wretched old troll was gone, and she would never again darken his life with her negativity. He walked to the kitchen and poured himself a glass of bourbon. Going into the living room, he sat back in his comfy old recliner and kicked up his feet. He raised his glass for a moment. "Here's to you, you hateful old bitch. I hope you're roasting somewhere," John said aloud. As he put the glass to his lips and began to sip, he heard his piano begin to play.

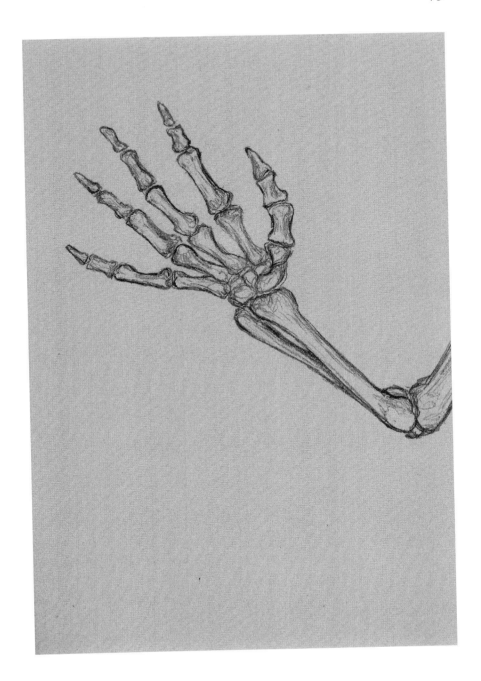

The cemetery, all alone,

A midnight stroll,

Is where he found me.

At first sight of him,

I trembled,

But then there was calm,

A peace I'd never known.

It felt as though,

We were one,

Although we'd just met.

He reached for me,

I did not turn away,

And as he tightened his embrace,

I leaned into him.

His voice was low,

And surprisingly soft,

As he said to me,

"I have found you at last.

You are now mine."

I closed my eyes,

A sudden chill,

Raced through my body,

As though someone,

Had walked on my grave.

As I opened my eyes again,

The world seemed to fade,

As did he,

Into the night.

It was as if I'd dreamt him,

As though my heart,

And my longing,

Had caused him to be.

Desire

Crossing the grand ballroom, I feel him watching me.

I am caught in his stare; I dare not move.

I remain still, breath bated,

Awaiting his approach.

In a blink, he stands before me.

His eyes of onyx drinking in the sight of me,

He softly nibbles his own bottom lip,

Head slightly tilted,

A devilish grin emerging,

From his sweet yet devious mouth.

He leans in and whispers into my ear,

"Come play in the shadows."

His voice is like velvet.

I possess no resistance, and so I follow,

Out into the black of night.

We cross the moonlit lawn,

And enter another part of the manor.

It seems we are alone in this darkened wing.

He leads me to a chamber lit faintly by dancing flames.

Beautiful candles of all shapes and sizes.

As I walk towards the window to take a peek at the night,

I hear him close the heavy wooden door behind us.

He is instantly at my back by the window.

I feel him there, but see no reflection of him in the glass.

He slowly traces one slender finger down my spine.

His face is against my hair.

He inhales me so deeply.

"Shall we play, love?"

I feel I am a hollow doll, unable to move or speak.

A pretty little doll for the taking.

He turns me to face him, his body pressing against mine.

My heart thunders inside its cage,

And my breath has become rapid.

Before I realize what is happening, his soft lips are upon my own.

I let myself go, falling into this delicious kiss.

A deep, entrancing kiss that conjures dark promises,

And an appetite for things forbidden.

His fingers find the satin ribbon lacing the front of my gown,

And nimbly untying the bow,

The ribbon floats gently to the floor by our feet.

I stand before him, exposed.

A sight unseen by any man.

But I feel no shame, only excitement.

The rush of sweet sin.

I realize I long for him to touch me,

I need to feel his hands upon my naked flesh.

His lips press to mine again,

Then he traces a soft line downward,

His mouth and his hands in a tandem dance,

Across my breasts,

Until I feel the sensation of electricity,

Pulsing throughout my body.

Suddenly, he pulls his face away,

And, panting, stares into my eyes.

He forces me backwards a few steps,

Until I'm up against the stone wall.

I feel the rough cold of it on my bare skin…

…It feels so primal…

With an almost invisible hand,

He effortlessly removes,

The remaining fabric from my body.

I hear the sound,

Of his own clothes being undone,

Though I dare not look.

He clutches my chin in his hand,

And raises my face so I can see,

All…all of him,

As he stands before me,

A sultry paradigm of beckoning danger.

A small gasp catches in my throat.

"I…I have never…"

My voice trails off,

Both from fear and sheer anticipation.

His beautiful lips again betray that devilish smile,

"I know," is all he says.

He lifts me up,

My legs instinctively encircle his waist.

He slides into me, and I stifle a small scream.

He is not gentle, but also not brutal.

No, it is an exquisite pain,

Such as I have never felt before.

Our bodies find a hedonistic rhythm.

Ecstasy escapes me in voluminous moans.

I feel as though I might lose consciousness.

He wraps his fist into my raven hair,

And pulls to expose my delicate neck,

Into which he sinks his dangerous bite.

I begin to tremble at my very core,

The juxtaposition of sensations,

So very dizzying:

Him thrusting powerfully into me,

As the blood flows from my vein,

And into his lovely mouth.

Waves of rapture begin to pulse through our entwined bodies,

I cry out in uncontrollable passion,

He throws back his head,

Releasing a deep, seductive growl,

His tantalizing lips,

Still wet with my crimson essence.

The air around us,

Becomes as still as death.

I collect myself,

While he does the same.

My ladylike appearance,

Now feels false,

For I have crossed a threshold.

What would become of me now,

Once we leave this room?

I reach for my neck,

As my senses return,

And hurry over to the mirror on the far wall.

Expecting wounded flesh,

I am surprised to find,

Nothing but smooth, alabaster skin.

Then his breath is on my cheek,

Although he reflects not in the mirror before me,

And he bids me follow him again.

As we exit the room,

Every candle goes out,

Engulfing us in quiet darkness.

I walk softly behind him,

Out once again into the moonlight,

Crossing the plush lawn.

He stops just outside,

The large outer doors of the ballroom,

And turns to take my hand.

Kissing it tenderly,

He smiles the same devilish smile,

As when we first met.

He then raises his arm and mine,

Twirling me, as if we are dancing,

Spinning me through the open doors,

Into the grand gathering of revelers.

Around and around,

I feel almost dizzy,

And stop to turn back and find him,

But he is not there.

I glance anxiously about the room,

To no avail,

As he has simply disappeared.

My heart sinks into a pit,

No one has even noticed,

That I had stolen away at all.

My mysterious lover has vanished,

Like a mist after a hot rain,

And I wonder curiously,

If I had imagined him somehow?

The stroke of midnight,

Finds me awake in my bed,

Unable to forget the night,

The passion and the fear,

He had driven into my soul.

I rise and cross the room,

To the open window,

I stand there, breathing in the night,

As he had breathed me in,

A cool breeze dancing along my skin,

Reminding me of the stone wall at my back,

I tremble, recalling the feeling,

Of him inside me,

Of his touch on my body,

Of his lips on my neck,

Of his piercing bite.

The wind shifts slightly,

And upon the haunting air,

I hear a faint voice whisper,

"Come play in the shadows."

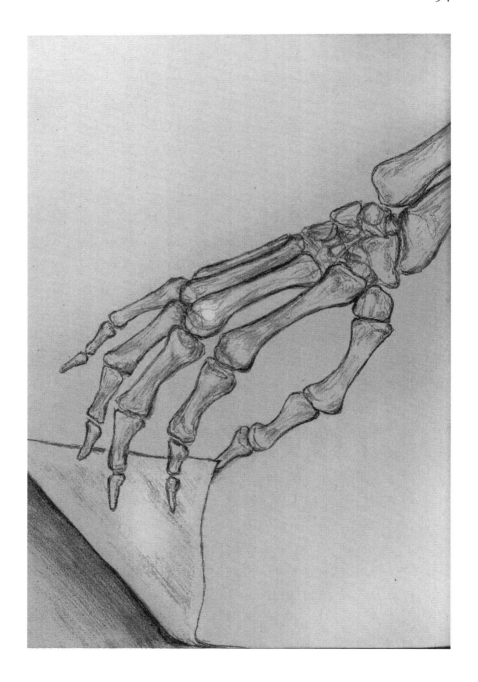

Hazy, twisted shades of grey,

Rain drizzles down from above,

Like crooked, bony fingers tapping against my skin.

I look out over the slabs of stone,

As the wind begins to tousle my hair,

I feel a presence other than my own.

The cemetery is awash in silence,

Save for the rain and the wind,

And the slow release of my bated breath.

A dark figure looms in the distance,

But it seems to be moving closer,

At a quickened pace that causes me some alarm.

No features appear as it moves closer,

It remains dark and mysterious,

Making no sound as it glides along the ground.

The dark figure is upon me now,

I close my eyes and feel nothing,

I open them to see I am again alone.

No figure stands before me nor behind,

No sound except the rain and the wind,

And my now gasping breath.

I turn to leave the cemetery,

And meet the empty gaze of the dark one.

Grave

"There's something on the grave."

I stopped in my tracks,

In the middle of the cold, rainy cemetery,

And turned back towards the dampened,

Fresh plot from which we had just walked.

"What do you mean?"

I looked back,

Through the mid-morning fog,

Trying to see,

If something was there.

"That. Standing *on* the grave."

It was a tall, black shape,

Slender and somewhat human-like,

And it seemed to be standing,

Directly on top of the loose dirt.

"I will go give it a look."

I made my way back,

Through the bone yard,

Stepping carefully between,

The stones of finality.

"Be careful!"

Of what should I be frightened?

It is probably just a mourner,

Distraught as are we,

Numb and unaware of proximity.

"The fog is no doubt affecting our sight."

Up the slight incline,

Of the slippery hill,

I slowly approached the figure,

Yet still could not decipher what I saw.

"Excuse me, are you alright?"

I receive no visible or audible response,

I am but a few feet away.

Do I call out again,

And disturb this stranger?

"Who are you talking to?"

I turn to see the priest,

Who had walked back to the graveside,

Once the crowd had departed,

To see that all was as it should be.

"That mourner standing near the grave."

And yet, as I turned,

My eyes could detect no one,

Not a solitary soul within reach,

No one upon the grave.

"Grief can be troublesome. Get some rest."

I turned to make my way,

Back through the cemetery,

As the gentle rain returned,

I could have sworn…

"What did you find?"

There was nothing to tell,

Simply our imaginations,

Or some trick of the light,

Combined with our sadness.

      "Let's head home now."

I took my seat in the carriage,

And as the horses began to pull,

I looked out my window, seeing a sight

That made me whisper to myself:

      "There's something on the grave."

The wind is chilled,

And the sky is black,

I know for me,

There's no turning back.

The gravestones around me,

Cast shadows of gloom,

And branches are creaking,

Like scratches from tombs.

The chill of the night,

Makes its way to my bones,

I stand in the silence,

Afraid and alone.

A whisper of danger,

The threat of demise,

The thought that I won't live,

To see the sunrise.

An unnatural howl,

Pierces the night,

My own body shudders,

Riddled with fright.

The sound of panting,

Heavy breath at my neck,

I turn with a feeling,

Of instant regret.

Before me is standing,

A beast of great size.

It has sharp, deadly fangs,

And hungry, red eyes.

With motion suspended,

I stand helplessly,

Awaiting this creature's,

Devouring of me.

Whether from panic,

Or from absolute fright,

I fade into darkness,

And awake in the light.

The creature has vanished,

My life has been spared,

Or so one would think,

But if they only dared,

To look into my eyes,

To search deep for my soul,

I'm afraid they would find,

I have lost all control.

No longer am I,

The person I was,

The human who cared,

The one who was loved.

A change has occurred,

My soul made anew,

I'm a creature of the night now,

And I'm coming for you.

Delight

Please, do come in.

You must be chilled to the bone.

Come inside my parlor; the fire is warm and delightful.

How was your journey?

Few are willing to travel this far,

Particularly at this late hour.

Are you hungry? I could have something brought up.

No doubt, you are in need of a drink.

You must try this wine,

For it is most delicious.

This chalice was believed to be,

From the court of Charlemagne.

I do love how the deep red rubies,

Take on an almost sanguine hue,

Against the smooth silver.

Drink up, love. Enjoy.

I shall gladly pour you another,

As we while away the evening,

Indulging in one another's charms.

Yes, relax now. Your pulse has slowed,

And your guard is down.

You tantalize me with your smile.

I don't receive many visitors,

Being so far from the village,

With no family to speak of.

How fortunate, then, that you lost your way,

On this dreadful night,

And found a path to me.

Have another drink, pet.

We have all night.

The fire is far from dying,

As am I.

You seem so strong and so delicate,

All at once; it excites me,

And I imagine what you taste like.

Oh, yes, this wine is quite strong,

And I am certain you now feel,

Somewhat fuzzy minded.

Have just one more, I insist.

Has anyone ever told you,

How deeply blue your eyes appear,

Against your alabaster skin?

Allow me to stroke your cheek,

And feel the softness of your hair.

Yes, you may kiss me.

I've thought of nothing else,

Since the moment our eyes met,

As you knocked upon my door.

Ah, yes. You taste as sweet as I imagined,

With lips as soft as satin,

And a pulse that quickens with every touch.

Wrap me in your embrace, love,

As my mouth finds its way down your chin,

And onto your neck, now exposed.

Trust me. I won't hurt you.

I drink you in, tasting the mixture,

Of your blood with my own.

That was not wine, you see.

Hush now, my dear pet.

Hold me as we become one.

Your soft moans turn from shock to pleasure,

As I drink you in,

And you feel reborn.

There, there. Relax, love.

Sleep now. I command it.

For when you awaken,

You shall be forever mine.

Nothing is what it seems,

We dance with death but do not ask its name.

Are we so certain that whatever lurks in the shadows,

Is the creature to be feared?

Or is it those that walk among us?

Be careful, lest you lose your way…

…And your head.

Escape

It was late, nearly midnight, just on the outskirts of the city. Darcy hurried along the street, trying not to draw too much attention. She was always hearing how it wasn't safe out here this time of night, especially for a young woman walking all alone. Darcy wasn't afraid tonight, though. No, she was more annoyed because the walk from her place over to the location of her friend's party was quite long and took her through a couple of back alleys. Darcy hated back alleys. They always reeked of urine and garbage. People could be so disgusting.

She crossed at a corner and walked past a group of men loitering outside a bodega. One of them was smoking a cigar. The aroma was nauseating to Darcy. "Girl like you shouldn't be out here all alone," bellowed the smoker with a laugh as she walked away. Darcy didn't look back, but she did hear the men begin to discuss how hot she apparently was. "Lovely," she said aloud to herself. "If I can't score tonight, I can just grab an old bodega guy on my way home." She rolled her eyes at the thought. She looked at her watch. "Damn. I swear, next time I should just stay home."

Darcy finally made it to the party around 12:45am. People were already wasted, but things still seemed to be going strong. She made her way through the crowd of strangers currently trashing her friend's house. A smile hit her lips when she finally saw a familiar face. "Emily!" Darcy waved at her friend from a doorway. "Darcy! Hey, girl! I was beginning to think you weren't going to make it tonight," Emily said as they embraced. Darcy looked around the room. "Who are all these people? I don't see anybody I know," she said. Emily shook her head. "They're people who apparently know Axl," she replied with a shrug.

Axl was really Alexander Xavier Larson. His parents had been huge fans of some band in the 80s, so they had purposely made his initials match the lead singer's name and had always called him such. Darcy always thought it looked misspelled. "Speak of the devil," someone shouted as Emily and Darcy felt someone's arms wrap around their shoulders from behind. They both spun around to see Axl grinning at them. "Axl!" shouted Darcy, hugging him. "The one and only," he replied. "Glad you could grace us with your presence, madam." Darcy laughed. "I like to be fashionably late is all." Axl stepped aside, and with a sweeping gesture, pointed to the quiet guy standing beside him. "Ladies, this is Bradley." He smiled, shyly. "So," said Emily, "You're not named after some rock star?" They all laughed as Axl made a face. "No, just plain old Bradley," he replied as his eyes met Darcy's. She felt herself smiling uncontrollably. "I'm Emily, and this gorgeous young thing is Darcy," said Emily, almost singing Darcy's name. "I'm afraid I must steal our host away. Why don't you kids go mingle?" Darcy shot Emily a look, but she was already locking arms with Axl and walking away.

"I guess we're supposed to get acquainted now," Bradley uttered. "Feel free to slip out of the room. I won't tell," he whispered. Darcy laughed. "Honestly, you're the only person here I feel I could have an intelligent conversation with," she said. Typically, Darcy would have made some excuse and bolted.

There was just something about this guy, though. She felt drawn to him, and was curious to learn more about who he was. She spent the next two hours on a couch in Axl's downstairs game room talking to Bradley and losing track of time. They seemed to have a lot in common. He was genuine, and he had class. He wasn't trying to make a move on her, hadn't even attempted a kiss. They had literally just been talking the entire time.

Suddenly, Darcy felt a very familiar feeling in the pit of her stomach. Her head began to ache. "Um…I have to go. I'm sorry." She stood up quickly. So did Bradley. "Are you okay? Can I do anything?" His concern was all over his face. "No, I just need to go home now. It's nothing serious. I promise," Darcy said as she attempted a smile. "Tell Axl and Emily I will catch up with them tomorrow night." She turned to leave, but turned back and held out her cell phone. "Here, put your number in," she demanded, but in a sweet tone. Bradley quickly obliged. Darcy called the number he had entered and heard a soft little musical tone coming from his pocket. Bradley grabbed his phone.

"There," she said, "Now you have mine, too." She gave him a wink and dashed out of the party before he had a chance to object.

Darcy hurried back in the direction of her place. How could she have been so stupid? How could she have stayed so long at that party? She knew the rules. She knew what she had to do to survive. Chatting at a party with some cute guy wasn't it. Her head began to pound furiously. She felt weak. "Dammit," she uttered under her breath. She looked around. The dark streets seemed deserted. Where were people when you actually wanted them around? She hurried towards the bodega on the corner. Oddly enough, two of those horny old men were still out there. Including cigar guy. Darcy hurried past, just like before, only this time she caught eye contact with the smoker. "There's my little lady. Where you running off to, girl?" If Darcy rolled her eyes any harder, they would pop out. She quickly made her way across the street, and she was certain she heard footsteps fall in behind her. About midway down the block, she carefully glanced back. Yep, there he was. Old cigar guy was following her.

Darcy's mind began to race. Where should she go? She hadn't really had any sort of plan in mind, what with her headache and uneasy stomach. "Damn," she exclaimed. At the next corner, she turned left. This street went down past her favorite clothing store. A hole in the wall place that only locals knew about. She made a mental note to stop by there tomorrow night. She heard footsteps and chanced another glance back. Cigar guy was still on her heels. Darcy knew there was a dark alley coming up, so she quickened her pace and turned into it suddenly. She rushed back to the very back of the alley and hid in the shadows. After about thirty seconds, cigar guy came strolling into view.

"Where did you go, little girl? You can't hide from me. Come on, I'll make sure you get home nice and safe, cutie pie." His voice made Darcy cringe. She could see him in full view, now. He was looking around for her while rubbing his privates.

What an absolute sicko. Darcy took in a deep breath, exhaled slowly, and walked out into the light. "Whoops. You found me. Whatever shall I do now?" Her sarcasm was noticeable. "Why don't you walk over here and let me show you, little girl? You know you want it," said cigar guy. Darcy wasn't afraid. No, she was smiling. She tilted her head. "Okay. Have it your way." With a devilish grin, she lunged for the man right there in the alley.

"Get away from her!" The voice bellowed out of nowhere. Suddenly Darcy felt someone reach between her and the cigar guy with a great force. She fell backwards onto the pavement in the alley. Stunned, she looked up to see Bradley grabbing cigar guy by his shirt. She watched helplessly as it dawned on Bradley that cigar guy was dead. His neck was punctured and his shirt, soaked in blood. Bradley let go of the shirt and cigar guy's lifeless body slumped to the ground. He stumbled back a few steps. "Wh-what the hell? Darcy?" he stammered. He turned and saw her sitting on the pavement. "Darcy! You wouldn't let me drive you. I wanted to make sure you got home okay. He was following you. I don't understand. What happened? Are you okay?" Bradley's bewilderment was palpable. Darcy stood up slowly, dusting herself off in the process. "Oh, Bradley. You shouldn't have come." He walked over and grasped her hands. "Are you okay? Are you hurt?" Darcy shook her head, still looking at the ground. "I really liked you. You shouldn't have come. Why did you have to follow me?" Darcy raised her head, her gaze meeting Bradley's. Her pupils were red, and for the first time, Bradley became aware of the fangs in her mouth. Fangs that were dripping with blood.

"I…I was worried about you. I wanted to protect you," he said. Darcy shook her head. "I had to feed. That's why I left so quickly. If you just could have left it alone….but now I can't risk anyone finding out. You might tell Emily, or Axl. We can't have that, now, can we?" She stepped closer to Bradley. A look of horror came over his face. "Darcy, wait. I won't tell. I promise. Just please-" "That's what they all say," she replied, then she lunged forward and sank her fangs into his throat.

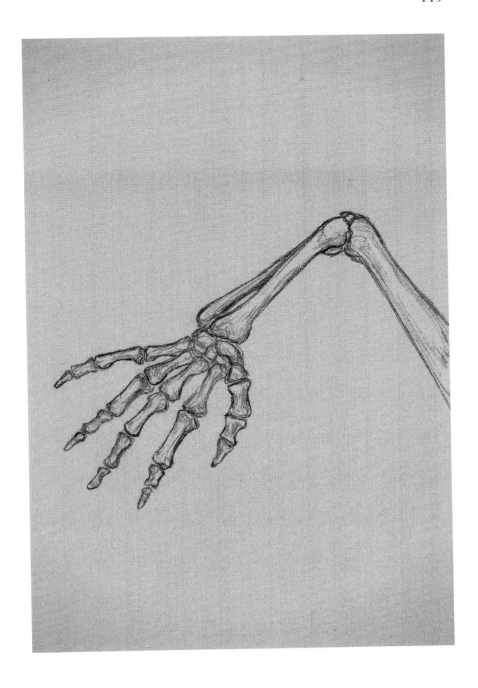

I can hear the rain.

The storm brewing outside,

Stirs within my soul,

And makes my heart dance.

What chilling things shall this night storm bring?

Wind lashes the trees,

With a slow, guttural growl,

Like a transparent Machiavelli.

Bellows of thunder rattle the panes.

Rain begins to hit harder now,

Tapping against the windows,

Like the bony fingers of an impatient ghoul.

Bright light flashes through the darkened room.

The lightning announces itself,

Like a cracking whip,

Tearing through the dismal clouds above.

The room is dark once again.

I light the popping, crackling fire,

Wood hissing like dark serpents,

As flaming reflections fill my eyes.

The storm is a thing of beauty.

A witch's brew of chaos and peace,

All the elements crashing together,

Until all that is left is the silence of the night.

Keeper

The tiny droplets of rain danced delicately along the spider's exquisite web. A slight, post-storm breeze shook them gently, making them appear more like glitter than water. Like tiny little sparkles. Kasey had always liked that word: *sparkle.* She didn't really know why; it had just always appealed to her. She watched as the spider slowly began to repair the damage to part of the web. Sometimes it was so peaceful and fascinating to watch little creatures doing mundane things. She began to lose herself in the simplicity of it all. That's when a loud voice bellowed from inside the house, piercing the tranquility.

"Kasey! Get off that damn porch and go help your mama with the dishes!" That was Kasey's dad. He was an angry man who honestly had no business being a father. He had never wanted any children, a fact he repeatedly made known to Kasey and her mom whenever the opportunity presented itself. He hated his life, he hated his family, and whatever job he was barely holding on to at the time. Kasey could smell the alcohol emanating off him as she walked by his recliner. The man had zero coping skills other than drinking excessively and beating his wife and daughter. What a sight he was, consumed by rage and drowning himself in an elixir of pity and pain. He made every day hell for Kasey. "Out there daydreaming like a goddamn baby! Dreams won't do you any good in this world, little girl! I can promise you that!" He always had to kick someone when they were already down. Kasey didn't dare respond. She knew better. Her verbal defenses were no match for his fists.

Kasey walked up beside her mother at the sink. She reached into the water and picked up a dish to rinse. Her mom nudged her gently with her elbow. "He doesn't mean it, dear. He's just had a rough day. Ignore him," she said. That was always her mantra: he didn't mean it. Kasey wanted to say, "I guess he didn't mean it when he bruised your cheek yesterday, either, huh?" She didn't say that, though. She just bit her lip and stared into the soapy water. They continued washing the dishes together in silence. Once the kitchen was tidy, Kasey headed upstairs to get ready for bed. It was still a little early in the night, but she was exhausted. A difficult home life will do that to you, especially at fifteen. A little while later, her mom came in to say goodnight. Kasey hugged her tightly. "Got all your homework done?" Kasey leaned back and looked at her with a soft smile. "Yes, mama. I did it all at school." Her mom returned the smile. Kasey wanted so badly to ask her mom why she didn't just leave him, and why she put up with things the way they were. She had so much to say, but all she managed was, "Goodnight, mama. I love you." She lay there for some time, trying to drift off to sleep. Her brain was not cooperating tonight. It kept replaying her dad's hateful words from earlier. Suddenly, the yelling wasn't just in her head anymore. An argument had erupted downstairs. This was not uncommon. Thankfully, she didn't hear any crashing around this time, just yelling. Kasey rolled over on her side and cried herself to sleep.

Shortly before midnight, Kasey awoke for no apparent reason. The house was eerily quiet. She tried to drift off again, but her brain was not having it. She thought she heard a soft noise by the window and went over to investigate. Nothing was out there. Just the dark of night. She decided to go downstairs for a drink of water. She was careful not to make noise, lest she incur the wrath of her father. All that man needed was a reason, and she always tried her best not to give him one. On her way back to the stairs, she decided to step out onto the porch for a quick breath of night air. Kasey loved the night. It always felt so peaceful. She stood on the porch with her arms wrapped around herself against the breeze. The moon was a crescent sliver in the darkness. She closed her eyes and felt the air on her skin. The night was so calming. She opened her eyes again, and just as she was about to turn to go inside, she noticed movement. Out at the edge of the woods, something shadowy had caught her attention. Kasey rubbed her eyes, blinked a few times, and looked again. Now she wasn't so sure anything was there. It had been tall, too tall to be a deer. A person? She walked to the edge of the porch and looked again. She was almost leaning.

"What in the damn hell are you doing out here in your nightgown? You want the neighbors to think you're some kind of a whore?" Kasey's heart stopped as she began to turn back towards the door. It all seemed to happen in slow motion. The realization that her dad was awake and out on the porch with her. The sound of his angry footsteps across the wooden boards as she was turning her head. The far-away sound of her mom's pleas for mercy. The stinging slap of his hand across her face, nearly knocking her backwards off the porch. In a daze, Kasey felt herself being yanked up by one arm. He was dragging her back into the house now. The front door slammed shut. He threw her into a heap at the base of the stairs. "I ain't raising no slut! Who were you out there talking to? Are you sneaking boys in my goddamn house?"

His angry face hung over her own so closely that she could feel spittle from his lips hitting her cheek. Kasey tried to respond. All she could manage was a whisper. "There was nobody, daddy. I was alone out there. I thought I saw-" He shook her violently before she could finish the sentence. "Don't lie to me, goddammit! You think I'm some kind of fool? Next time I catch you out whorin' I'll break your legs!" For added emphasis, he kicked her swiftly in the stomach. As he walked back to bed she heard him say, "You ain't acting like a whore in my goddamn house." Her mom knelt down next to her and held her, both of them crying. "Oh, Kasey. Baby I'm so sorry. I couldn't stop him." Kasey choked back the bile rising in her throat. "I just want to go back to bed, mama." She helped Kasey to her feet and back up to her bed.

The next day Kasey did her best to hide the bruise on her face. Luckily, the other bruises were hidden by her clothes. People didn't really notice her to begin with, so it wasn't that difficult to pretend she was okay. The school day went by in a blur, and all too soon she found herself back at home. It was only half past three in the afternoon, but her mom was already cooking dinner. "Mom? Are we eating early?" Her mom gave her a soft smile as she eased a pan of chicken into the oven. "Yes. Your father has a poker game tonight at six, so he wants to have dinner when he gets home." Kasey knew that on Fridays her dad always got home around 4:30pm. She loved the reprieve she got during poker nights, but dreaded the end of them. When her dad got home late he was either the happy drunk who won and wanted to celebrate, or the angry drunk who lost and was looking for someone to take it out on. She helped her mom in the kitchen and at 4:37pm they were all sitting down to dinner.

After her dad left, Kasey began to help clear the table. "No, no, honey. You let me worry about that. Go do something for yourself," chided her mother, although lovingly. Kasey knew this was her way of saying sorry for the night before. Kasey went upstairs and finished up her homework. She didn't want it hanging over her all weekend. After sunset, she found herself back out on the porch. Her spider friend had vanished, the web no doubt a casualty to the melee the night before. No more sparkle. It seemed as though anything good in her life was fleeting. She scribbled down some random thoughts in her composition notebook. She didn't dare keep an actual diary. No one needed proof of what she actually thought around here. She found writing poems cathartic. She could be abstract enough that no one would know what or whom she was writing about.

She stayed out there until it was too dark to see without the porchlight. She never used it, because it attracted too many bugs. She closed up her notebook, gathered her pen and her glass of water, and stood to go into the house. A flash of something made her look back. Out there, by the edge of the woods. She was almost certain there had been...no, it couldn't have been. She strained to get a better view. Nothing. No shadows, no animals, nothing. Kasey tried to rationalize the glowing red eyes she had glimpsed at the edge of the trees. Trick of the light? She rolled her eyes at her own thought. What light? It was dark! Maybe some weird lightning bug or something? Nothing out here had red eyes. Whatever it was had been too tall to be an animal. Kasey settled on bugs. It had been bugs that made her think she'd seen red eyes out there in the darkness. She went back into the house and headed upstairs. She wanted to be asleep before her dad got home.

The screams woke Kasey in an instant. Her first thought was her mom. He was beating her mom. Then she realized the screams were coming from a man. A man outside the house. Kasey threw on her robe and ran down the stairs. Her mom was just running out of her bedroom. "Kasey? Honey, was that you? Are you alright?" Kasey clung to her mom. "No, mama. It wasn't me. It came from outside." She looked around the dark, quiet house. "Where's dad?" Her mom put her hand over Kasey's lips to quiet her and whispered, "He hasn't come home yet." More screams, closer this time. They both realized that it sounded like Kasey's dad. Her mom's eyes widened in horror. "Oh my god!" She nearly broke the door flinging it open, and she and Kasey ran out across the porch and on to the lawn. Kasey saw her dad's brown boot, part of his coat, and his wallet all just lying there. The screams sounded as though he should be right there, too, but he wasn't. Then they suddenly faded into thin air. Her mom was screaming now. Kasey looked over and followed her mother's gaze to the ground around them. It was saturated with a deep crimson hue. "Kasey, get back in the house!" Her mom grabbed her and ran with her back inside, slamming the door and locking it tight.

The rest of the night was a cacophony of sirens and questions. The public explanation was large game. Some wild beast attacked her father as he was walking through the yard. Kasey didn't believe that, though. She would have, but she overheard the sheriff saying how there were absolutely no tracks except for her father's. No evidence of a corpse. It was as though he had been plucked up into the sky. Her mom was obviously distraught. He was a monster, but somehow she had loved him anyway. Kasey didn't share her mom's grief. She was relieved. He was finally gone. No more beatings, no more yelling, no more baseless accusations. When the fervor downstairs had begun to subside, Kasey finally crawled into her bed. For the first time in her life, she had no fear. She closed her eyes and began to slip into a most delicious, deep sleep. She never saw the two red eyes watching over her through the window.

Steal me away from this place,

And take me to the land of darkened dreams,

Where we can frolic among the graves,

Waking the dead from their slumber.

The cool night breeze,

Carries the faintest odor,

Of frankincense and rotting flesh,

Such a sweet and intoxicating mix.

Dark clouds above us,

Begin to sprinkle us with rain,

Let's dance naked in the rising mist,

As the creatures of the night take flight.

Your eyes meet mine,

And I can see such a seductive evil,

And a mysterious grin,

That alludes to an exciting horror.

A chaotic place full of broken toys,

Lollipop daggers and belladonna potions,

And carnival rides,

That only go in reverse.

You lead me towards the deranged souls,

Playing the wicked games,

In which madness is the grand prize,

And everyone wins.

Tryst

The demon whispered, "Come dance with me, little girl."

I blushed, and turned to hide my face.

"No, no. Don't hide from me. Show me everything."

He pulled me into a tight embrace.

I looked up into his eyes, black as the inside of a grave.

His stare was so intense; I thought he might kiss me.

Then his breath was on the side of my neck.

It was hot, but it sent a shiver down my spine.

He brushed his lips across my skin, and whispered.

I strained to hear.

"You smell so sweet."

He pressed his mouth to my neck again, as his hands began to

roam my body.

I was lost in the sin of it all.

Without warning, he grabbed me by the throat.

He walked me backwards to the bed.

His stare was deep and dark.

His brow, furrowed; his grin, lupine.

"Down."

I heeded his command, and lay back across the bed.

The demon climbed on top of me.

I was naked and vulnerable under his weight.

As I stared into his ebony eyes, he ran his claws delicately up my torso.

I bit my lip, suppressing a moan.

With both his hands, he gripped mine at either side of my head.

He pressed his mouth onto mine, his forked tongue ever teasing.

As I began to tremble with anxious anticipation, his grip on me tightened.

He lowered his mouth between my neck and shoulder and bit down.

I cried out, and he laughed onto my skin.

The mixture of pleasure and pain was almost overwhelming.

His lips brushed my ear, and he whispered, "You are mine. Always. Whenever I want you."

I let go of the breath I had been unconsciously holding, and opened my eyes.

He was gone.

I was alone in the night, naked and trembling.

In the faint distance of the darkness, I heard his laughter.

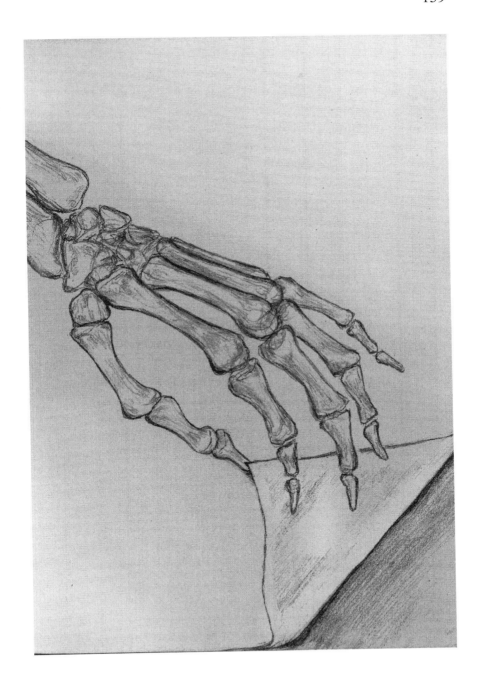

Outcasts are often created,

By those who don't open their minds.

They would rather be collectively cruel,

Than reach out a hand and be kind.

Rumor can outweigh the truth,

When people discriminate so,

Curiosity should not lead to fear,

Of that which we do not know.

Whispers and wonder abound,

But those who are curious ask not.

Remember, we all shall be equal,

When we lie in the ground, left to rot.

Revenant

When they found her body out in the field, many assumed it was some type of ritual gone awry. Yes, there had been blood, but maybe she was using that to contact some dark entity? The rumors began to fly. She was someone that everyone in town knew *of,* but knew nothing *about.* She kept to herself and seemed to prefer the company of animals to that of other humans. As people are wont to do, the blanks were filled in with whatever suited the imagination. Words like "witch" and "dark magic" were often thrown around when she was the topic of discussion. There were folks who truly believed she consorted with the devil himself and the souls of the damned.

The local authorities decided an investigation was not warranted. She was simply a disturbed individual who kept to herself and walked the path of the occult. What did she expect, dealing with supernatural forces? Her death was ruled a suicide and she was unceremoniously buried in the very field where she had been found. Her given name had been Lydia, but the entire town had nicknamed her with various derogatory distinctions. According to the locals, she wore jewelry made of animal bones and an eccentric top hat she stole from a voodoo priest. She supposedly lured animals to her yard not out of love, but to sacrifice them. None of this was ever proven, but in a small town like this, rumors take precedence over facts. After her death, she became nothing more than fodder for the folklore mill. Most had all but forgotten about her. About a month passed before the wailing began.

The townsfolk near the field were awakened one night by the most awful wailing. It sounded as if someone or something was being brutally murdered. Men grabbed their guns and ran outside towards the ghastly sound. A crowd had gathered, presenting lanterns and rifles, but they could find no source for the noises. However, the wailing continued. "Somebody go call on the sheriff. Get him out here!" shouted one of the men. A young farmhand ran to the nearby stables and mounted his horse. As he rode off into the haunting night, he could still hear the wailing as though whoever or whatever was making that sound was riding alongside him. Not long after the farmhand had left, an apparition began to appear near the source of the wailing. The crowd of men all stumbled back, startled and frightened. One even fired his rifle, but it passed through the apparition and struck another man in the left arm. "Hold your fire!" was shouted by several in the crowd. They all stood helplessly and watched as the apparition took shape. An animal? No, a person. A *woman.* She was average height, with long hair and a tattered shroud of a dress. As the face began to materialize, they all realized who they were looking at. This…this was *Lydia.*

By this time, the women had ventured out into the darkness to check on their men. The crowd around the apparition grew larger, everyone staring in disbelief at the sight before them. The wailing continued, and suddenly Lydia began to move forward. She almost seemed to be gliding across the ground, each step taking her farther than a natural step should. The terrified crowd parted as she passed through them, all the while wailing like a banshee.

She lifted her arms as though she was reaching for something or someone in front of her, and she slowly made her way down the darkened road towards the center of town. The crowd hesitantly began to follow.

Just before the procession reached the center of the town, the farmhand came galloping up with the sheriff close behind. The sight of this macabre parade stopped them both in their tracks. The sheriff bellowed, "Just what in hell is going on out here?" As they dismounted, Lydia came within about twenty feet of the sheriff. Just then, she stopped. So did that horrible wailing. The crowd grew eerily silent. The sheriff stared at her, or rather *through* her. He looked to the crowd, and then back to the apparition. When the sheriff realized what, or more accurately *who,* he was looking at, he became frozen in absolute fear. Lydia tilted her head slowly to one side, her mouth curving into a sinister grin. "You," she said. "Tell them the truth."

Everyone was confused by this. What truth? What was she trying to say? The sheriff began to shake his head, his eyes wide with disbelief and shock. He wanted to run, but his feet felt as though they were staked to the ground. He simply muttered, "It…it can't be…" and then he trailed off. Lydia's face went from mischievous to pure rage. In a flash, where her ghostly flesh had been, there was now just the bone beneath. A sinister skull with eyes for revenge. "TELL THEM!" She quickly lunged forward, closing the gap between them until her face was directly in front of his, her mouth agape and a maddening scream erupting from it. Her hair seemed to float around her face as if blown by a violent wind, yet the air on this night was still and silent. The sheriff visibly tried to shrink back from her demonic shout. Lydia's hand darted out and wrapped around his throat. He began to choke. She tilted her head the other way. "Hmmmmm?" she said. With the last breath left in his lungs, the sheriff managed to whisper, "It was me." Lydia dropped him in a heap at her feet. He was gasping for air now. He looked up to see an angry and confused crowd looking back at him. Tears flooded his eyes as he drew himself up onto all fours, coughing and gasping. "It was me. I killed her. I killed Lydia. It was an accident, though, I swear to God!" One of the local deputies spoke up then. "What do you mean, an accident? What did you do, Hank?" The sheriff tried to lift himself to his feet, but Lydia let out a deep growl. He stayed on all fours. He continued his tale through choked sobs.

He had been at the local tavern after his shift ended, drowning his sorrows in a bottomless tumbler of cheap whiskey. The town election was only a few months away, but his opponent was already ahead in popularity by a landslide. His career could be over, then what would he do? It didn't help that his wife of 32 years had left him two nights prior. She had been having an affair with a blacksmith in the next town over, and now she was saying she no longer loved Hank. Yesterday he had lost more money at the poker game than he could really afford to. The barkeep reluctantly poured him another drink. He wasn't about to argue with the sheriff, lest he risk trouble for his business. He was also aware of the troubles the sheriff had been having.

"Who did you piss off, Sheriff? You've had a right sorry string of bad luck," he said. The sheriff just shook his head and took another drink. A man sitting two stools away overheard their conversation and piped up, "Maybe that old witch has it in for you?" The sheriff and the barkeep looked up at him, confused. "Who?" asked the sheriff. "That witch. The crazy old bat that lives out by that empty field. I bet she done put a curse on you, sheriff." The barkeep told the man to mind his own business, and the sheriff just drank on in silence. Later, he left the tavern and drunkenly began the ride home. He nearly fell off his horse three times. When he reached his house, he rode right past. He couldn't bear the thought of going into that empty house all alone. He rode down the old dirt lane aimlessly, his drunken thoughts building his rage.

By the time he reached that empty field, missing his wife had turned into hating her. Kicking himself for losing his money became being certain the others had been cheating. A movement in the shadows caught his eye from across the field. Was that…..it was. Scary old bitch in her stupid hat. Maybe she really was a witch? Hank had had several run-ins with her. As far as he was concerned, she was a blemish on this town's reputation. Always arguing with local hunters and stirring up trouble. She wasn't a proper woman, no husband or children. Just did whatever she damn well pleased. Maybe that kind of attitude is what caused his wife to leave. Maybe this Lydia woman was a witch after all. If she had cursed him, she would pay for it. He slowly dismounted his horse and began to cross through the darkened field. He took his revolver from his holster and slowly cocked the hammer. There she was. Was she dancing? She might be taking down laundry…no, she had to be dancing. Probably naked, doing some sort of devil worship. Hank's rage finally got the best of him. Now he had someone in front of him to take it out on. He raised his gun, and took a step forward. A small twig snapped under his foot, and Lydia turned around. The bedspread she had in her hands fell to the ground. Hank's hands shook with misguided hatred. "You….you cursed me, woman!" His words were slurred. Lydia put her hands up in a gesture of pleading as well as defense. "Sheriff? I don't know what's going on, but I haven't done anything to you," she said gently. Hank steadied his hand and closed one eye. "Don't lie to me, bitch," he grumbled. Then the gun went off.

The bullet grazed her shoulder, and Lydia fell backwards. Fear overcame her and she found herself unable to scream. Hank lunged forward and grabbed her by the hair. "You ruined my life!" he shouted. With extreme force, he slammed her into the tree. Her head made a cracking sound as it hit the wood. She tumbled back onto the ground, blood trickling down from her forehead. He stood over her body for what felt like hours. She looked so innocent now, so harmless. The blood from her head was now pooling with the blood from her shoulder. As the whiskey wore off, he began to feel guilt and fear. What would he do? How would he explain this? Maybe he didn't have to. With the last shreds of liquid courage coursing through his veins, he concocted a cover story. He took his knife and made cuts all over her body. He found some chicken in her kitchen and tore out the bones, scattering them on the ground around her. Last, he lit the fire pit for just a few minutes, long enough to make fresh ash. Before he left, he smeared some ash on her face, for good measure.

After he finished his story, he collapsed to the ground. "I couldn't tell anybody. I panicked....I....I made it look like some ritual or something. Figured nobody would question it. I didn't mean to...I'm sorry!"

With those words, Lydia's face flashed from skull to ghostly, alabaster flesh again. She turned towards the crowd. Raising her arms out to her sides, she said softly, "You are *all* to blame. He may have ended my life, but none of you ever questioned the circumstances of my death. You preferred your fables to my truth. I will have my revenge upon you all, for once you return to the weeds and your corpse is in the boneyard, you will find me waiting there. I will bring upon you all the most grisly, dreadful nightmares for all eternity. If the living cross those cemetery gates after dark, I may very well take their souls while they scream." With that, she turned and began to walk silently towards the cemetery gates. As she passed by the sheriff, she placed her hand gently under his chin and lifted, causing him to slowly rise to his feet. For a few seconds, they seemed to exchange knowing looks. Then she turned and continued her walk, the sheriff following listlessly behind her. As they reached the gate, she stepped aside and let him walk in first. As she stepped inside and began to close the gate, she looked up at the crowd once more. She lowered her chin slightly, and the sinister grin returned. She placed the top hat gently on her head, slightly to the right. Her face again changed from flesh to bone, and with a wicked laugh, she slammed the gates shut.

The sheriff's body was found the next day, and he was buried in his family plot on the north end of the cemetery. The townsfolk went back to the field to exhume Lydia's corpse, planning to give her a proper burial as well. Her makeshift grave was empty. To this day, no one knows what happened to her body. Some say she still roams the cemetery each night, ushering souls into the afterlife; some with hospitality, others with vengeance. The townsfolk eventually gave her the name Madam Mortis. She is considered the dark queen of the cemetery. Rumor has it, if you find yourself within those decrepit old walls after dark, she will gladly give you the grand tour. Whether or not you make it out alive is entirely at her discretion.

In the dead of night,

When the moon disappears,

Behind ominous clouds,

That bring shadows and fear,

Under a blanket,

Of silence and gloom,

The souls of the restless,

Shall rise from their tombs.

Deep in the darkness,

The creatures of night,

Awake from their slumber,

And prepare to take flight.

Whispers are carried,

Upon the cool breeze,

Like a graceful danseuse,

Through the cemetery trees.

The cries of a spectre,

Echo from within,

The cold, marble walls,

Of the old mausoleum.

The air holds the stench,

Of death and decay,

The devils await,

To help prolong your stay.

The caskets are rotting,

The corpses are freed.

The graves are disturbed,

And the demons will feed.

The end does not come,

When you take your last breath,

For inside this graveyard,

There is life after death!

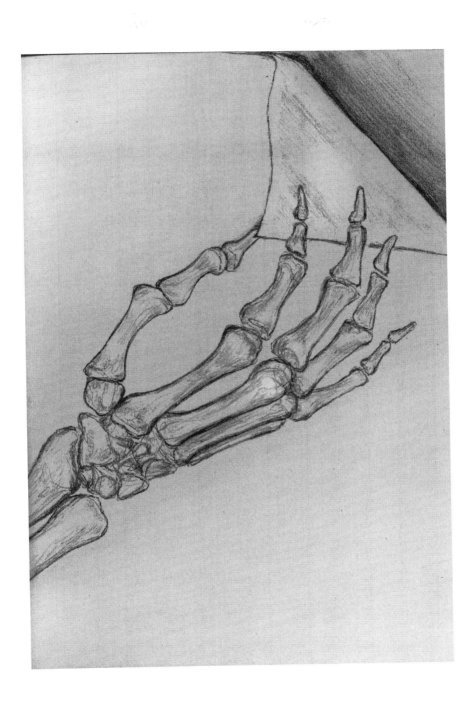

Author's note: Some of the stories in this book contained controversial subject matter. I do not write about these types of things lightly; some of these characters and situations were created out of my own personal experiences. If you are struggling with anything, be it depression, abuse, suicidal thoughts, or anything at all, please know you are not alone. Reach out to someone. Here are some valuable resources:

National Suicide Prevention Lifeline

1-800-273-8255

suicidepreventionlifeline.org

Childhelp National Child Abuse Hotline

1-800-4-A-CHILD or 1-800-422-4453

www.childhelp.org

Substance Abuse and Mental Health Services Administration

1-800-662-HELP or 1-800-662-4537

www.samhsa.gov

You can also reach out to me anytime via my **Twisted Libra** website. I have email and social media links there, and I am always willing to listen. Never think you are alone.

www.twistedlibracemetery.com

Made in the USA
Columbia, SC
01 November 2020

23825653R00087